MIGRATIONS

Short fiction

Kathryn Holzman

Picaflor Press

CONTENTS

INTRODUCTION

My grandfather on my father's side was a man of few words. My vivacious Norwegian grandmother was the one I adored. When I threatened to run away, she was the one I always planned to run to. Grandpa was simply background. Never ruffled, he smiled when Grandma disappeared into a bar during a family road trip forcing us all to sit in the stifling car while my father retrieved her. I have trouble recalling his voice and only remember his customary expression of detached bemusement. When my cousin and I decided, at the age of four, to get married, my grandfather presided over our exchange of vows. I did not know his own father had been a judge of some repute. He never spoke of his background. It was my mother who told us that my soft-spoken grandfather came from an illustrious Oregon family with buildings named after his ancestors at both the University of Oregon and the University of Washington. My grandfather, like my father, my brother and my son, was an engineer, an unexciting profession to a young girl who aspired to be a writer, an artist, and a lifelong rebel against the middle class. By the time I knew them, my grandparents lived a quiet life supported by a comfortable pension which my grandfather received after a long career at Graybar Electronics in downtown Seattle.

In a family box of photos, I discovered a portrait of my grandfather as a young man. Taken in 1908, the picture reflected the times, but in so ways it also spoke to me.

I studied my grandfather's expression looking for stories that had never been told. My mother, always tuned in to the family gossip, told me that my grandfather had been divorced early in the century. Long before he met my grandmother, at a time when such things were not discussed. Despite the tease of scandal, she could tell me nothing more.

After my father died, I immersed myself in my family's genealogy. I found a biography of my great, great grandfather, the geologist, on Google books. I read old newspapers articles, both the yellowing pages that I inherited and others available via the internet. To my delight, I read through family archives, three boxes of memorabilia maintained by the University of Oregon.

As I read, I looked for passion among relics of propriety, humanity amid of the pride of history. While I was impressed to discover a letter from President Taft inviting my great-great-grandfather to the White House, a brief newspaper notice announcing my grandfather's first marriage thrilled me.

There is no other record of my grandfather's first marriage, no wedding invitation or announcement has been preserved. But I found a name and googled my grandfather's first wife. A nickname: Lulu. I discovered a life, a poet, a librarian who never remarried, a fellow writer.

This chapbook is a collection of stories inspired by migrations, the migration of my ancestors to the west. My parent's migration from Seattle to California when California was new and our sub-division replaced bucolic acres of apricot orchards. My own migration east to NYC as a 21-year-old fleeing a fractured relationship with my parents that resulted in my dropping out of college.

Many of these stories grew from research I did on my family's genealogy. But more than the facts I uncovered as I did this research, these stories came alive with the questions that remained. Did the Geologist, my great-great-grandfather, wonder if his descendants would one day see his signature deep in a cave in Oregon? Did my grandfather ever tell his second wife about his first? Why could my mother never leave behind the abandonment she felt as a child? What did she mean when she told me "If I had had a choice, I would not have become a mother."

This is the territory of fiction. Rooted in the real world, my characters wander. I do my best to follow them. As a daughter, sister, and mother, I know that every member of a family has their own truth. No two of us see our past in the same way. This is my truth, but in its creation, I try on another's skin and explore the misinterpretations that so often divide us.

Kathryn Holzman, 2016

MIGRATIONS

Heading east, the Amtrak train barrels across the open plains of Kansas on a sultry August night. A young couple dozes on a dusty seat. They are still wearing the clothes they had put on the night of their departure from Seattle. Kenny, his long hair a tangle of curls, his jeans stained with stringy holes at the knee, sleeps with his girlfriend Kathy wrapped around him like a blanket. His backpack, their only luggage, bounces on the metal rack above their heads. The couple smell of patchouli and marijuana. As the train stutters and slows, Kenny whimpers, lost in a dream of red lights, of police cars outside his boyhood home. "Kenny, are you all right?" Kathy asks. Her plump, pink arms cushion him like a pillow. She watches as he struggles to wake up, rocking him until a glimmer of recognition crosses his face. The train has come to an unexplained halt. They are in the middle of nowhere.

Heading west through the dead summer air, a young Methodist minister walks towards the train, erect beside a prairie schooner wagon, one in a long line of wagons. He is a beacon of propriety among the malodorous oxen and seasoned fur traders who accompany him. The minister's long beard elongates his face; his piercing eyes give him an air of certainty.

The vehicles meet in an open field. Their occupants step

out into the dead summer air, yawning and stretching, muscles stiff with fatigue. The minister scratches a stick into the dry Kansas soil to analyze its composition. His wife, pale and woozy with early pregnancy, climbs down from the covered wagon. She nods away her husband's offer of assistance and accepts a tin cup of water from traders while gazing up at the stars as if looking for a map. The trappers treat her with respect, making room for her in front of the campfire they have already built in the field.

Both couples eye the other without comprehension. They rub their eyes to confirm the vision unfolding before them. Needing to rest, the wagon train's oxen graze, weary from labor and wary of the "gee" and "haw" of their drivers' snapping whips.

Kenny and Kathy steer clear of the pioneers, leery of their strange clothes, of their primitive mode of transportation. Empowered by the first flush of love, they cling to each other even at this moment of collision. "We're almost there," Kenny says to Kathy, licking her ear. "New York City, skyscrapers and everything." They are dead set on tasting the "sexual revolution." Late one sex-filled night in Seattle, they read an article in Newsweek describing the burgeoning nightclub scene in the city, and together they giggled at the possibilities of pansexuality. They have $500 and endless possibilities.

The Minister attempts to distract his wife from the spectacle of the embracing couple. A student of geology born near a limestone quarry in Ireland, he is traveling to a mission just east of Mount Hood on the Columbia River in Oregon. The lure of unsettled land and rocks fascinate him. "Here, my dear," he says as he settles his wife on a wool blanket which he has spread on top of the dry grasses.

Kathy perches on a boulder nearby. She gawks at the pioneers. In the brown clarity of the minister's eyes, she sees her own parents' condemnation. In response, she throws her leg over that of her lover. Out of the corner of half-shut eyes, she dares him to watch her. Pulling Kenny down next to her, she guides her lover's hand to the inside of her thigh, sweeping her long, tangled hair from her face. Kenny lights a joint which she sucks on, eager.

The train idles in the field. The lives stock tied to the wagon train ruminate on the grass of the prairie. Everyone here is ready for respite. Pulling out a hand-drawn map prepared by settlers who had preceded him, the minister approaches the disheveled couple as they perch on the boulder. "Greetings, strangers. What brings you to this field on this glorious, starry night?"

He introduces himself. "My name is Scott." Close up, the two men realize they are about the same age despite the differences in their attire and appearance. Without waiting for a response, Scott pulls out his map. He shows Kenny the route he is following, an "x" marking his destination. Kenny bends over and examines the map, curious to know where the minister is traveling.

"The Oregon Trail is being carved out by fur trappers and traders," Scott says. "Our route passes here through the lower Platte River Valley near Fort Kearny and then through the Rocky Mountains. In Walla Walla, Washington, we'll board a boat to purchase supplies before crossing the Snake River in Oregon's Blue Mountains. We will continue west until we reach The Dalles."

Scott traces the journey on the hand-drawn map. His fingernails are short and clean. Kenny has bit his to the quick. He shares details of his own trip, pulling out a wrinkled Amtrak schedule which he has jammed into his jeans' pocket. "They call our train," he points to the Amtrak idling on the far side of the field, "the Empire Builder. It travels from Seattle to Chicago. From there, we'll board the Lake Shore Limited. Twenty hours later we will arrive at Pennsylvania Station." Kenny takes another toke off his joint and offers it to the minister. "New York City," he says with a dramatic sweep of the hand holding the cigarette, "where anything is possible."

Unfamiliar with the tobacco his new companion is smoking, Scott refuses the man's offer. "I've heard of Iron Horses which will one day carry trains across our Union," he studies the schedule with fascination. "I have never had the fortune to see such a marvel!" Even at this darkest hour of the night, lights glow within the idled cars. He examines the train with the discerning eye of a scientist. "New York, you say? When I first emigrated from Ireland, I lived in New York with my family. We traveled on horseback."

Left on her own, Kathy untangles her hair with dirty fingertips and sweeps it back from her face before joining Scott's wife at the campfire. Smoke irritates her eyes. The trappers view her suspiciously. When a scruffy man winks at her, she winks back and attempts to stare him down.

The trapper, redolent of tobacco and livestock, approaches the two women. "What do we have here?" he asks, reaching for Kathy's bare arm. "A well-fed lass you are," he ogles her ample breasts.

Kathy glares back. "Keep your hands to yourself, old man."

He lifts those hands, rough and calloused, preparing to respond in undisguised anger. The minister's wife inserts herself between them, putting a protective arm around her and pulling her close. In a soft voice, she cautions the trapper. "There will be no more of that." The trapper looks at the minister's wife, her long gingham dress, her swelling belly, and withdraws his hand. Issuing a mumbled apology. He slinks away into the darkness.

"The nerve," Kathy says as he disappears, but she covers the other woman's hand with her own, still shaking. The two women sit together for a moment, hand in hand in front of the fire.

"My name is Constance," the minister's wife says.

"I don't need your protection," Kathy withdraws her hand.

"We all need one another," Constance replies.

Kathy changes the subject. "I hear you're going to Oregon. You will love it," She stretches out her legs. They both gaze at her worn leather sandals. "I went to an amazing rave in Portland just last month. Oregon is amazing."

Constance does not understand what the wild-haired woman is talking about, but she knows a lost soul when she sees one. "Where are you bound?" she asks. Tucking her long skirt beneath her, she apologizes for the iron stains on her petticoats which she is attempting to hide." Keeping clean on this journey is an everyday struggle." She shifts and sighs. Kathy's cutoffs are frayed, stained, and smell of urine and menstrual blood.

Scott and Kenny join the women at the fire pit. "These people are traveling to New York City," Scott tells his wife as he seats himself next to her, his eyes bright with the possibility of sharing new companionship. In the distance, trappers are spreading out thin, fold-up mattresses, blankets, and pillows under the stars. A few tents are being erected–one of these prepared for the Minister and his wife.

"Do you have family in New York?" Constance asks.

"God, no. We're leaving all that behind. The plan is to crash with a friend in her NYU dorm room until we can get a place of our own."

"It's a sad day when you leave family behind," Constance rests her hand on her bulging belly. "The open plains of our journey are often so desolate." As the minister's wife looks to her husband for comfort, Kathy looks down, registering the woman's baby bump.

"Shit, you're pregnant." Kathy can't imagine.

"The Lord watches over us." Scott replies.

Kathy doesn't even try to bite her tongue. "That's easy for you to say! You're not the one who is going to give birth in the middle of nowhere." She points at the sanctimonious minister before stretching her arms over her head in to release the spasm her indignation had triggered. "You pompous prick."

Scott doesn't even flinch. He welcomes any opportunity to preach. "You think you are far from home, in a strange land with a strange people. But you are mistaken. Friends and family are always with you."

"Bullshit." Kenny lights another joint. "Ties that bind. They'll choke you every time."

Kathy agrees. "The point is; we don't need family. That's the goal. We're here to make a new beginning." She challenges the preacher, enraged by his smugness.

Scott, ever the scientist, replies, "There are no new beginnings."

Constance looks up at him with sweet resignation.

Kathy guffaws. "Spare me your solicitude."

Not one to give up, the preacher counters. "From the earliest fossils our lives are a continuum. We only have to discover the connections."

Kathy guffaws. "Yeah, as if." He reminds her of the professors she left behind, swept away by their own self-importance and oblivious to the disruptions about to change the world as they know it.

"I'm just along for the ride." Kenny yawns, losing interest in the debate as a wave of desire and intoxication overcomes him. He passes the joint to Kathy who inhales and then looks him in the blood-shot eye.

"You are everything we are trying to escape," she says to the minister.

The minister reaches out for the cigarette, accepting the unlikely peace pipe as any cautious traveler would.

Kathy watches him inhale. He does not pass the joint on to his wife, but returns it to Kenny. He does not look at her but directs his engaging smile at Kenny, who smiles back, as delighted as a puppy.

They continue to smoke. The smoke of the campfire envelopes them; the absurdity of their situation delights them. They can hardly contain their mirth.

When sleep overtakes Constance, the minister pulls her to his side, his broad shoulders supporting her slender frame. "I had better let my wife get some sleep. I pray that your journey is fruitful." He hugs Kenny goodbye, holds Kathy in his piercing gaze as if to burn his image into her memory.

Kathy and Kenny watch the strange man disappear into the dark night.

"Wow, that was weird," Kathy says to Kenny. As they walk back to the train, she is ravenous and chews on a granola bar Kenny retrieves from their backpack. "Keeping clean on this journey is an everyday struggle," Kathy mimics, swishing her invisible skirts. Scott makes fun of the pioneers' stodgy attire and the preacher's pompous if well-meaning words. "Friends and family are always with you," Scott says, assuming the man's erect posture, imitating his intense stare, emulating his air of certainty.

In the dark train they make silent love and then drift off

into a sleep populated by ghosts. In his dream, Kenny once again watches his mother as she climbs up onto the railing of the Tacoma Bridge and then floats down, splashing into the water and disappearing from his life. That night, as every night, he cries out in terror and Kathy holds his shaking body, stroking his head with reassurance. In his face, she now seeks a resemblance. That night as they sleep in each other's arms, she offers him comfort. As she does so, she feels the warmth of the minister's wife's arms around them both.

In the morning, the wagon train bustles with activity as trappers prepare the pack animals to resume their journey. The train conductor announces that the Empire Builder will resume its travels east in half an hour. The engine snorts with impatience and the passengers return from the field. The pioneers pack up the bedding and put on their heavy boots. The train travelers sit up straighter and stare out the windows with one last look of wonder.

And then the migrations resume.

The pioneers continue westward as the train chugs to the east.

By the end of the week, Kenny and Kathy arrive in New York where the University security guard kicks them out of the dorm. That first night, they sleep in a morning mist on the roof of the dorm. Far above it all, stars wink at them through the haze of city smog.

SHOES

Last night Marta dreamed that she had forgotten to wear shoes again. This happened all the time. She headed to work and realized that she was barefoot. Sometimes she looked for a shoe store on the way to the office, figuring she could buy some cheap ballet flats that would get her through the day. Other times she just kept her feet under the desk and hoped no one would notice.

Marta was raised in a warm climate, so these dreams never caused her physical distress, just embarrassment. The need to conceal her feet was the driving emotion. Now that she had moved to New York City, she had additional concerns.

The morning she left the City, Marta put on a pair of practical black pumps in need of polish. The kind of shoes no one noticed.

Women paid unbelievable amounts of money to teeter on uncomfortable heels. Marta couldn't fathom why anyone would pay $750 for Jimmy Choo's. Her inability to understand their appeal made her wonder if she belonged in the City. Her roommate, Diana, took great pleasure in shopping although she never paid retail.

Marta began working as a bookkeeper at the Lotus Company, a New York City importer of Asian goods, right after she graduated with a degree in Finance. The company resold replicas of museum-quality pottery made for the Imperial Court to high-end department stores in Manhattan. Marta expected to be underemployed but accepted the job because the post promised trips to China.

Her boss, Lydia, was an overweight and overbearing

woman with hair dyed an implausible shade of red. Lydia's much older and extremely wealthy husband had passed away after a heart attack ten years earlier and had left her the family company and an all-encompassing sense of entitlement. She wore elegant and expansive silk brocade shifts, each handmade by a custom tailor with shoes dyed to match. Marta worked out of Lydia's apartment in a high rise on the East Side of Manhattan. Her responsibilities were not well defined. In addition to the books, she ran errands and provided a less than sympathetic ear to her employer who had an endless litany of aches, pains, and situations in which she felt she had been taken advantage of.

Marta's roommate refused to fix her up with friends of her many friends; she told Marta she over-analyzed. Her boss, Lydia, who dismissed her frequent requests for a raise, told her that she was short-sighted. In the end it didn't matter. She kept meticulous books, a talent that secured her livelihood. She thought of life as a puzzle and she excelled at puzzles.

The numbers were the easy part.

Lydia dangled the promise of foreign travel and raises that never came. She was pleased with Marta's work and within months promoted her to Assistant. The promotion came without a change in salary or working conditions. She still expected Marta to pick up her personal prescriptions, a task which filled Marta with resentment.

Marta and Diana lived in a midtown residence for women. The location was good, the rent reasonable. They had a cozy room with double beds, a small refrigerator and sink. When they had first moved in, both new to the City, they had not realized that Bellevue Hospital used the hotel as a transitional residence for psychiatric patients after discharge. The residents shared a bathroom in the hallway. To minimize danger, the roommates never drank water before going to bed.

Diana loved Manhattan. She developed an offbeat sense of style and cruised resale stores for underpriced items, gently used designer clothes, trendy platform shoes. She often went out after work to drink with office mates. She sang Karaoke and slept with men she had just met. On those nights, Marta was alone at the residence, often feeling too uncomfortable to leave her room. Instead she went over Lydia's books and realized that she didn't need to wait for Lydia to give her a raise. It was all a matter of credits and debits.

Whenever Diana came home drunk, Marta put her to bed, removing her shoes and tucking her in. Most mornings, the roommates shared coffee, bagels and, for Diana, aspirin. Marta regaled Diana with stories about Lydia's confrontations with her building's doorman whom she felt did not guard the high rise with sufficient vigilance. She confided in her roommate, lamenting the late night phone calls from her boss who expected her to be on call at all times. In turn, Diana described her latest conquests, providing just enough detail that Marta felt that she, too, had been out on the town. Diana was content living in New York; Marta wanted to travel.

To ease her mind, Marta bought a book that suggested interpretations for common dreams. She developed a fear of forgetting to put on items of clothing. In the hallway outside her room, she sometimes heard women talking to themselves. Paranoia was rampant among the building's residents. On the door next to theirs, the occupant had taped a sign for the exterminator which said *Don't kill me*. Down the hallway, a woman had single handedly moved her stove to block her door for safety.

The book about dreams said that nakedness could express fears of rejection. A dreamer might be naked in public where everyone laughed at her. Marta dismissed this explanation out of hand. To be rejected required a need for acceptance. Marta had Diana and a good job. Her academic record was solid, and her parents trusted her. No one was going to laugh at her.

A new lady named Rose moved in across the hall. She seemed sane, about the same age as Marta's mother, well-groomed if a little mousy. In the elevator, she had overheard that it was Marta's birthday and one evening she knocked on their door holding a package wrapped in birthday paper, a pretty peach-colored blouse in a lacy style more suited to a young girl than Marta. Over birthday cake, Rose chatted with the girls about life in New York. When Diana left for a rendezvous, Rose urged Marta to be a role model for Diana who she feared was going astray. Marta recommended that Rose avoid the shared bathroom at night.

The Lotus Company imported delicate ceramics from China, The profit margin was enormous. Twice each year, Lydia traveled to the Mainland to visit the factories where her goods were made. Over time, she had developed rapport with factory owners who were impressed by her size and obvious wealth. She named her price and never budged. Marta admired her boss's business acumen and enrolled in a night class in Mandarin to learn the art of haggling. Since math and language used the same centers in the brain, she was optimistic.

It fell to Marta to make the reservations for Lydia's trips and to keep the business going when her boss was away. Learning Chinese was a great help. She began to address the Chinese suppliers by name. In Lydia's absence, Marta became friendly with the Lotus Company's auditor, a junior accountant eager to please. After work, the two of them walked to the subway station and commiserated about the frustrations of working for Lydia.

After one of her business trips, Lydia gave Marta a set of fragile blue and white vases, a reward for all her effort. Marta placed them in the windowsill of her room, facing Third Avenue. Their fragile elegance only emphasized the shabbiness of the room's decor. Marta wanted more.

The book about dreams provided another explanation. Shame. *Are you afraid people will expose you?* Marta reviewed the Lotus Company's books with Alan. She understood his methodology. As long as there were valid invoices, he did not question Lydia's expenses.

Lydia had promised Marta a trip to China. The bank account that Marta opened would fulfill that promise. The invoices that Marta generated were for expenses that easily could have been valid; the names of the fabricated suppliers were generic and didn't merit a second glance. She did not feel ashamed. She had listened for hours to Lydia's accounts of her trips to the Orient. She knew the names and addresses of the luxury hotels where she stayed, the four-star restaurants where she ate. Lydia always traveled first class, a necessity she said for such a long flight.

Marta told Diana that she would be leaving for China soon. Diana had become involved with a married man. She now spent evenings drinking in high end restaurants and was seldom home before 2 a.m. Her married man whisked her away on weekends to Montauk. She truly thought he might leave his wife.

Rose never spoke about her own life or how she came to live in a woman's residence in Manhattan but there were always fresh flowers on her nightstand. She called Marta "Dear" and admired her commitment to her job and the long hours she worked, even at night in her room at the residence. She urged Marta to aspire to greater things. "Your boss should pay you more," she said, echoing Marta's own sentiments. Marta described Lydia's harassment of the factory owners who did not make their deadlines, her abuse of delivery boys, and the irrationality of her expectations. Some evenings when Marta's phone rang off the hook. Rose encouraged her to ignore it; she understood that Marta needed time away from Lydia's endless, petty demands.

The book said: "It is rare to be proud of being naked in your dreams, but when this occurs it is a very positive symbol." Marta's Chinese was coming along. Her teacher congratulated her on her aptitude. She was skimming just the right amount off the business, enough to fill her account without drawing Alan's attention. Lydia increasingly depended on her. Diana's married lover offered to pay for an apartment uptown. Although Marta often missed her roommate, she enjoyed Rose's companionship. She accepted Alan's invitation to dinner, but never let things get out of control.

"You should sleep with him," Diana advised her when Marta told her about Alan. "Make him complicit. He'll never turn on you then." They were drinking margaritas to celebrate their one-year anniversary in the City. Her friend's calculating attitude surprised Marta; she had thought of her roommate as shallow.

"Do you think Rose is married?" Marta wondered out loud.

"I wonder what her story is." Even before the words were out of her mouth, she realized that she was treading on shaky ground. Diana wouldn't want to talk about wives. She preferred to talk about Marta's frustrations on the job. The success of Jimmy Choo, she pointed out, could be attributed to the Vogue editor, Tamara Mellon, who took his company public. There was always somebody behind a company's success. Marta appreciated her encouragement. They ordered a second round of margaritas before returning to their room.

Later that night, Marta woke up to howling in the hallway. For a moment, she thought an injured animal had somehow made its way into the building. Instead, she realized, someone was weeping outside their door. With effort, she made out words amid the sobs: "Don't leave me." "Hold me," and saddest of all "I'm so sorry." Diana tiptoed to the peephole to see which wacko had lost it tonight.

"It's Rose," she reported in a theatrical whisper. "She's huddled outside our door, stark naked."

Marta pulled a blanket around her and joined her roommate at the door. Sure enough, Rose had assumed a fetal position on the flower-patterned carpet. Her jagged inhales fueled eerie wails of utter desperation. The pale specter of her body seemed never to have seen the sun.

"Shouldn't we help her?" she asked.

Diana was already calling 911. "Can you send someone up to the fifth floor, room 502, please?" Marta did not stop her. After all, what could they do?

"I'll miss you, sweet child," Rose sobbed when the EMTs arrived. Marta could not tell whether she looked towards their door as the medics pulled her away.

Like the other guests at the residence, they remained behind closed doors. Marta would never know if the spectators laughed as the medics sedated Rose, wrapped her in a hospital blanket and carted her away, never to return. Although Rose was clearly unstable, Marta wondered if Diana thought then of the man she was sleeping with, who had abandoned his wife. Did she ever worry about the pain she might be causing?

The book concluded that being naked in a dream revealed a fear of being exposed. Of course, being barefoot was far from being naked, Marta told herself. She almost never dreamed of leaving home without clothing. It was just shoes she sometimes forgot.

Marta was not one to judge Diana's choices. But she did not follow Diana's recommendation that she sleep with Alan. She had her eye on the bottom line. Nevertheless, Marta found it harder and harder to sleep at night. She was afraid her malfeasance would be discovered and dreaded running into the other ladies on the floor. She questioned her ability to assess sanity. At night, she dreamed that she walked along 2nd Avenue barefoot among a crush of businessmen. She feared what else might be missing if she looked down, her white body on display for all to see. The vision of Rose huddled in front of their door haunted her.

Diana laughed off Rose's meltdown. Just another crazy lady. Marta no longer felt comfortable confiding in her roommate. As a result, she felt lonely, out of place. The scuffed black flats were the least of it.

"Be good to yourself," Diana said to her the day she announced that she was moving uptown. "It's time to move on. I'll keep you posted," she promised. The exact words that Tamara Mellon tweeted the day that she resigned.

When Tamara Mellon left Jimmy Choo, the shoe company she helped to build, she reportedly received a payout of roughly $135 million. According to the New York Times, she left without explanation.

Marta, too, was getting ready to make her move.

The morning of her flight, she dressed carefully, checking twice to be sure that every item of clothing was in place: underwear, bra, blouse, and skirt. She wore opaque tights and her scuffed black pumps. Everything was as it should be. She settled the bill at the residence and left with a light heart.

Unlike Rose, she left on her own volition, head held high. When the TSA agent at the airport required her to remove her shoes for security clearance, she wasn't afraid of being exposed. Following Lydia's advice, she flew first class.

THE COST OF ELECTRICITY

In 1905, I eloped to Seattle with my college girlfriend. Three years later, my parents decided to announce my betrothal tastefully, as would befit the son of the Chief Justice of the Oregon Supreme Court. The commemorative portrait still brings me back to the tension of that weekend, my father's begrudging recognition of my new status, and his unspoken disapproval.

In the family portrait taken in 1908, the Judge stands front and center, his expression serious, his mouth framed by a drooping walrus mustache, bald pate shiny, white vest and dark suit. Beside him, mother's posture is perfect, her expression solemn. Her high, lacy neckline is the sole touch of adornment on her staid black dress. All five of us, dutiful sons, cluster around them in matching dark suits.

My wife, Lulu, brought the only light to the occasion. My father's mouth pursed every time she entered a room, but my brothers adored her. Her laughter filled my parents' parlor as we stood waiting for the photographer's flash powder to ignite. Lulu was a writer, formerly an instructor of English at the University, who always introduced herself to strangers and followed no rules but her own. which included dating her students (including me) and challenging authority (my father) for the thrill of it. Mother, as usual, was concerned with appearances. I must admit, the appearances weren't good.

My parents were the children of pioneers. As I attempted to introduce my wife to the assembled friends and relatives, my father lectured, as was his wont. He described the hardships he had experienced as a child, the bitter cold of those first winters in the West, the sorrow of siblings who died and the threat of Indian attacks. But, he concluded, the past is past and now is now. Even with the duties of a Circuit Judge, my father was an avid carpenter who spent hours creating perfectly beveled corners, dressers whose construction disappeared into perfect peg design. He sanded the surfaces in our home until the wood was flawless.

He expected no less of us.

"When you go to the university..." When we were young, the words opened any discussion of our future. We were, after all, his legacy, his best students, the inheritors of all he had achieved.

"The study of Law brings order to the wilderness."

How many times had my parents told the story about meeting as members of the first class of the University? Lulu listened while my father described being among the young men who arrived early each morning to light the wood stoves. The men would already be upstairs before women students arrived. It was important, she was to understand, that the women ascended the stairs without fear of an immodest sighting of ankle bared by a lifted skirt. My father took great pride in my mother's education. He smiled as my mother offered her guests another cup of tea.

I stood and listened, a dutiful son. I too attended the University. But by sophomore year, Lulu was always there, just in front of me as we climbed the stairs. The object of my affection did not require courtesy. I followed her. Breathlessly, I watched the lively swish of her petticoats as she pranced ahead, always taking care to reveal to me the pale flesh of her dainty ankles.

The conversation around the parlor that night kept reverting, as usual, to responsibilities—responsibilities to the new State, the University, the future of the West. My father held forth, his voice deep and resonate, a man of Law used to an audience.

Underneath the tablecloth, I poked my wife's ankle with the toe of my boot, anxious for the evening to end.

Lulu had inspired me to follow my dreams. This, to my father's great dismay, did not include the study of Law. Instead, entranced by the fledgling science of electricity, I graduated from the newly formed Department of Electrical Engineering. For me, there was never any choice. I was born the year that lights came on. In 1882 in Manhattan, the first 59 customers were supplied electric current. By the time the governor appointed my father to the Oregon Supreme Court, long distance power lines had been installed in Portland and an electric railroad operated in the county. I enrolled at the University a year after the discovery of alternate current. While my father institutionalized the established territories, I went in search of the future.

Lulu was everything my parents were not. From the moment we left for Seattle, my life had changed. I never missed my family. Our living room filled with the artists and suffragettes who Lulu collected during her explorations of the City. "Don't mind if I do," was the salon's motto, always followed by a wave of appreciative laughter. Lulu loved to dance. If I, who needed to rise early each morning, could not waltz her around our living room as music played on the gramophone, other partners were available, tipsy journalists, unemployed poets. Even her fellow suffragettes took her in their arms to give her a spin.

The nation's first municipally owned hydro project, Cedar River, was under construction. In dark offices, my colleagues and I were poised to deliver power. Once the Cedar River plant was completed, the new alternating current technology would enable the linkage of small, competing companies that now dotted the City into one massive network. The final connections that would light up the drizzly winter days for good.

My co-workers envied my life. When Lulu visited our office, they watched her with hungry eyes. She knew their names and remembered their birthdays. Introverted engineers all, they ate up her attention as I basked in that glory.

I had no desire to return to Oregon. My parents' home was dark and the formal dinners my mother prepared tasted of disappointment. "Your brother has been accepted to Johns Hopkins Medical School," my mother wrote to me in her weekly letter. My father sent me articles in which his name appeared, which described him as honest and steadfast in purpose. My mother said: "The Judge works late each night on his Opinion. I worry about his eyes."

As the Judge's reputation grew, it became important that his family reflect well on him. My mother explained to me in a carefully worded letter inviting us to the 1908 soiree that his autobiography, which he was already writing, needed to include his "bright and industrious issue." Her words were meant to make us feel welcome, but the summons was clear.

Lulu had no use for correctness. The night we received the invitation we fought. Lulu threw her journal to the floor, stomping around the living room. "I refuse to be a part of this sham."

"Lulu, this is important. It's an overture on their part." I could not match her vehemence, so I chose the calmness of reason.

"And what does that mean to me? I have no desire to be a part of your father's legacy."

For the hundredth time, she pointed out that the only profession she could claim was "at home." The alumni newsletter still sat beneath the parakeet's cage where she had placed it as a comment on the status it recorded.

"You are doing something you love. What about me?" she demanded.

"Lulu, you are the brilliant star that lights my life." Even my father would have recognized my honesty. He valued my mother's demure demeanor more. To him, a woman's value could be found in unadvertised intelligence and moral fortitude. Lulu demanded more.

"Balderdash." Lulu picked up her journal and held it out in

front of me. "I refuse to be swallowed by your illustrious family." She spit out "chattel," delivered "illustrious" with scorn. "I deserve a voice of my own." I recognized the slogans of her Suffragette friends. In February 1907, a large procession had taken place in London to advocate for women's rights. When Lulu read the newspaper reports aloud to me, her voice filled with rapture.

"Just this once." I was afraid to add, "For me." I knew better. The green and yellow parakeet trilled above the alumni newsletter, in the sunshine of our kitchen window. Lulu picked up her journal, not looking back at me, and went into the adjoining room where she sat at her desk, settling with an audible sigh.

Lulu attended the family soiree. Once there, she entranced my brothers, shook the hands of my parents' friends like a man, and looked the blushing academics in the eye. She listened to my father discuss the finer points of his defense with those who aspired to be his peers. She drank champagne and accepted toasts to our union. "Don't mind if I do," she said to the elderly professors who vied for her attention, but the words were sharper now. She flirted and bamboozled them all. It was a magnificent performance.

When we returned to Seattle, Lulu perfected an imitation of the "great man" (as she called my father). To the amusement of her coterie, she lifted her chin as she strutted across our living room and proclaimed, "We have brought the rule of Law to these savage lands." She editorialized with poetic aplomb, "What a bombastic bore. A "bloviating benefactor." It did not occur to me to come to my father's defense.

Only later did I realize that her venom was meant for me. After our trip to Oregon, our lives continued to diverge. The demand for power in the growing city required me to work longer and longer hours as sources of energy were discovered and new networks connected. We were building a grid to power the new Century. I was determined to have a role in the enterprise.

In 1909 the Judge's successfully argued his Opinion on the Equitable Allocation of Utilities (the details of which even I could not grasp) before the US Supreme Court. In recognition of this accomplishment, my father was appointed to the Federal Court. "It is a great responsibility," he wrote me on official government letterhead.

More and more, Lulu was out. When I arrived home after long days at work, I made my own supper. When she was in the apartment, she was busy, reading political tracts and, pencil in hand, filling her journals with meditations on the role of women in the twentieth century. She typed poems and stories late into the night which she submitted to magazines. She didn't come to bed until it was almost time for me to get up. On the evenings when she was not reading her works at coffee houses and in local libraries, she rode her new bicycle to Seattle's Arcade Building where she met with other impassioned women in cluttered, frenetic office space.

Lulu prepared a brochure to advertise the convention of women which was to take place during the Alaska-Yukon-Pacific Exposition. She piled copy and edited proofs on our kitchen table, leaving no room for plates or cutlery. When the "Suffrage Special" arrived at King Street Station, Lulu greeted the arriving women with a bright red ribbon wrapped around her wide-brimmed hat.

"Lulu, please take care," I pleaded. Threats of violence surrounded the grass roots movement. The newspapers were full of incidents, a woman murdered on the streets of Everett, hooligans throwing rocks at well-intended demonstrations.

"I'm not afraid," she replied, shaking off my concern, my embrace. She, who had never been self-conscious, courted publicity and could stand up to anyone. Certainly me.

Lulu didn't like to be challenged. We never discussed my family. We never discussed a family of our own. I knew that that would be a step too far.

When she was not at home, I played music more suited to meditation than dance. I read the newspaper, one step away from the activism that obsessed my wife. Despite the electric light, our apartment was less bright than it had been when we first lived in Seattle, smaller.

Meanwhile, the Cedar Rapids Hydro plant quickly became a City institution, and the demand for power continued to grow. In early 1910, the City Council created a separate lighting department. They offered me a supervisor's position at the newly established Seattle Light. Arriving home to an empty apartment, I looked out the window on the City which hummed with the same energy that filled me. Having no one else with whom I could share my news, I began a letter to my parents. "Today, they offered me a job with City Light..." I kept falling back on hackneyed phrases, like "honor" or "responsibility" which my father already owned. After several false starts, I left the letter out for Lulu to read whenever she came home.

Two weeks later Lulu left for a visit to Portland to meet with the City Editor of the Portland Press. "It's an opportunity to discuss the role of activism in political change," she explained as she packed her suitcase before heading to the train station without saying goodbye. She never returned to Seattle. Or to me.

In November, Washington State granted women the right to vote, breaking a 14-year gridlock in the national campaign. A banner was hung from City Hall proclaiming, "Women do not need the ballot. The ballot needs women!" Watching it wave in the wind, I could only think: Lulu did not need me. I, of course, still needed her. Even my work could not fill the emptiness she left in her wake.

I never discussed women's rights with my father. His rulings dealt with the finer points of Law, the provisions of ordinances and the codification of exceptions. His cases included epic battles between the burgeoning utilities and local governments, not romantic notions of freedom or human rights. Passion had no role in his decisions. My father allowed me the dignity of never having to explain Lulu's absence. We never discussed the shame of divorce. My mother's silence was as close to forgiveness of my moral lapse as I was about to receive.

My solitary life now centers on my job and the long walks I take through the city I have love. Seattle continues to grow around me, each year brighter, noisier. Often, I spend time at the public library, drawn to their collection of literary magazines. Lulu, I have learned, no longer signs her work using my last name.

STALKING THE BEATLES

Bobby sneered when Alice insisted that the whole family climb into their blue Belair station wagon to see the Beatles. The popular band was on their first visit to the United States. The San Jose Mercury News reported that the mop-tops from Liverpool were staying at a luxury hotel near the freeway. From the moment they made the turn off 101, Bobby could see the hotel's circular drive, crowded with masses of teenage girls bearing signs saying, "Paul, we love you."

Bobby was there under protest.

As always, his mom had a plan.

"Mom," Bobby said, "the Beatles aren't going to be able to pass through this mob."

"You're right," Alice said. She directed their father to drive to an unmarked rear entrance of the hotel. Amenable, Jack snaked the car through an alley used by maintenance men and hotel employees and parked next to a garbage dumpster at the rear of the hotel. Patty said she hoped that they had the inside track. Two other cars followed, evidently hoping that the family had knowledge that they did not.

The excursion was a waste of time, but Patty said that stalking the Beatles was way more exciting than their usual after-dinner fieldtrips. Most nights that summer, after his mother had loaded the dinner dishes into the dishwasher, Bobby had been forced into the station wagon while the family went to ogle the ashes of train wrecks, house fires, or plane crashes. Or his father would park the car beneath the runways at the San Jose airport, waiting for calamity but settling for the thunder of landing gear being lowered and reversed engines bringing the massive vehicle to a vehement halt.

"One thing you have to admit about your mother," Jack liked to say. "She makes life interesting."

Bobby didn't see the point.

"You can't lock yourself up in your room for the rest of your life," his mother said, giving him no option.

Tonight, Jack drove, as usual following Alice's directions. He held his cigarette outside the car window, content to go along for the ride.

The crowd was growing fast. From her perch in the backseat, Patty craned to see the band, every muscle taut with anticipation. Bobby could almost feel the heat of the mass of the bodies crushing against each other. His skin crawled.

"God, this is embarrassing."

They waited. At some point the roar of the crowd filled the air, intermixed with the wail of police sirens. A crescendo shook the ground, rattling the metal of the malodorous dumpster. It was happening. The arrival of the Beatles in America was a big, big deal. They were there.

Or as close as they would ever be.

Wildfires burned in the foothills of the Santa Cruz Mountains. On the next evening's drive, the family got as close to the disaster as the police allowed, finding dirt roads to bypass roadblocks. Smoke signaled the highest flames. The sky darkened and the acrid smell filled their nostrils. They tracked the progress of the fire, gauging who was winning, the flames or the fire squads.

"Never a dull day in the life of the Hopkins," their father said. "These are days you will remember."

Bobby hoped not.

When Jack took his hands off the steering wheel to light his cigarette, the car careened, hitting the curb before he gained control. "Dad!" Patty and Bobby called out in unison, afraid of crashing down the steep embankment as the car radio played "Close your eyes and I'll kiss you."

Bobby watched Patty. She closed her eyes and sang along with the car radio as if she, too, were at the Beatles concert, surrounded by her peers on the vanguard of a world ripe for change. With a minor revision, he could see that history was being made. It all added up.

The world as they knew it would never be the same.

REAL ESTATE

Last night I watched Johnny, the computer billionaire, compete on Dancing with the Stars. He is a large man now with a mischievous grin and gray beard. His dancing was not impressive. Heavy on his feet, he lacked a sense of rhythm. The judges eliminated him in the first round. In my real estate lawyer's waiting room, I once saw a picture of his home in People Magazine. Nestled in the Santa Cruz Mountains with a skyline view, six bedrooms, five bathrooms, three fireplaces and a wine cellar, the article described his house as "an abode full of light and warmth."

On paper I too am rich. This afternoon, at three p.m., I will sell my home at 1319 Picaflor Lane in Santa Clara, California, for $431,500. Our family home built on the fertile soil of a cleared apricot orchard in the Santa Clara Valley. In 1960, my father, recently transferred to Moffett Air Force Base, relocated our growing family off-base to live in civilian society. For the first time, we would no longer be military brats. He purchased a newly built three-bedroom ranch–style house on a quarter-acre lot for $30,000. When I was three, I remember watching my father, crew-cut and erect as the soldier he was, saw through the trunk of the two remaining fruit trees in our backyard. "Too sloppy," he said. "I'm not about to rake up rotten fruit."

My mother, his Japanese "war bride," pregnant at the time with the third of five children (I was number two and the first girl) did not protest--not surprising given that she spoke not a word of English. Floral arrangements, delicate arrangements of fragrant apricot blossoms collected from the backyard, would no longer adorn our dining room table.

Now, of course, this valley is known as Silicon Valley, ground zero for the internet age. Where I grew up, where my siblings grew up and gave birth to my nieces and nephews, so did Apple, Google, and Yahoo. With the explosive growth of these companies, we have all experienced unprecedented prosperity. Or so they say.

My nephew, Eddie, is driving me to the closing. I take a seat beside him in his BMW which he has waxed to a high sheen. The car smells new, redolent of maleness and fresh leather. I am glad to be at Eddie's side, surrounded by family on the day when our house is being handed over to strangers.

Eddie is the first son of my sister Kathy. Kathy, the family beauty, blessed with long straight black hair that to this day hangs to her waist. Although she is only two years younger, I have always been like a parent to her. In high school, Kathy ran with a wild crowd, Chicano sons of migrant laborers and football stars who dated cheerleaders but drove my sister to the dam to watch "submarine" races on Friday night. While my hands were full helping my overburdened mother, Kathy grew tough fast but never lost her sweetness.

She was pregnant with Eddie by her senior year of high school. In our Catholic household there was never a question about keeping the baby. To everyone's surprise, Eddie's Dad, Mike, stepped up and offered to marry Kathy. Mike had barely graduated from high school and planned to enlist in the military. Instead my father took out the first of many second mortgages on our house and bought him the gas station on the corner of Fremont and DeAnza Drive which he still runs to this day.

From the beginning I offered to babysit. While Kevin, my older brother, was off riding his tricycle with a manic determination to achieve maximum speed, my voiceless mother had handed me each her babies like the gift of a new doll. I took on the role, proud to demonstrate my value to my father during his infrequent furloughs at home. My mother's inability to communicate set her apart. I followed his lead in shielding her from the demands of our growing family. By the time Kathy began her own family, this was the only role I knew.

Eddie was a good baby. At nine, he began studying judo and ju-jitsu. He was a natural. Our whole gang cheered him on as he pro-gressed from yellow belt, to brown and, by sixth grade, to black belt. My father, the military man, admired the discipline required by martial arts and, whenever he was in town, sat in his pilot's uniform in the front row with the other students' parents. "Atta boy," he would cheer on his grandson, never needing to raise his voice. Our family filled the first two rows.

I do not believe that Eddie ever hurt a child. He believes in dis-cipline, just like my Dad. I've watched him with his own infants; his gentleness is remarkable. In the martial arts, bamboo poles are used to hold a student's attention. A light tap here, a nudge there. Students blossom under this instruction.

My Dad had always been a hero. My mother was only the first of his rescues. In 1975, Hank D. Richards, 23, died when his A-7E Corsair crashed at an altitude of 4,200 ft. in a mountainous area about 10 miles north of Crater Lake while on a routine training flight. Dad responded to the crash. He was the same with us, al-ways there when we needed him, appearing just as we were about to crash. My mother became unmoored when my father died on a military mission in Southeast Asia. About that same time, Kathy spent a short stint in alcohol rehab (financed by another home loan backed by our house). Kathy came back from the edge. My mother never did.

But by them, Eddie had pretty much raised himself. In high school, he accepted an assistant instructor's position in the Mountain View recreation department's martial arts program, instructing the art of Hombu-style aikido. For five years now he has been teaching at his own Dojo. His students commend his exemplary, hands-on style, his straightforward skill. His wife Jo-anna is a former student.

The children that Eddie teaches are not the offspring of mili-tary men. Their parents are newly wealthy employees. Number one, two and twenty-five of multi-billion dollar internet start-ups. They do not want their children to be touched. They do not respect an instructor's authority.

The San Jose Mercury News called the lawsuit a nuisance, but not until reiterating the accusations of intentional and repeated child abuse for all to read. Eddie could lose his livelihood if the Dojo goes into foreclosure. By selling the house, I will save him.

I have been cleaning out the house for months now. Empty, the rooms are still full of memories. During my childhood, our house always teetered on the verge of chaos. The boys inherited Dad's mechanical aptitude. Cars in various stages of repair perpetually cluttered our driveway. When Dad was home, he lectured on car mechanics over open hoods, smoking a cigarette while instructing Kevin, and Jeff how to change oil, rotate tires, and adjust valves. Their hands were always greasy. Even little Joey observed from his parked stroller. My mother and I could never keep ahead of the next onslaught of hungry boys and thirsty teenagers with their grasping, greedy fingers. When Dad left for his next assignment, the boys drifted off, drawn away by sports and later girlfriends, but the cars remained, their hoods still open, their tires flat.

For the girls, dress-up evolved into Spin the Bottle. Kathy and I, joined by Jennifer from next door, dressed up in layers, as many as we could manage, hoop skirts, taffeta cocktail dresses, boas. We would spin a coke bottle. Wherever the bottle pointed, a girl removed one piece of clothing. The neighborhood boys jumped outside the bedroom window, hoping for a glimpse. The last to remain clothed won, but the excitement was always the slow titillation, the first blouse removed, the first white underpants revealed. As our finery piled up in the closet's corner, we blushed, self-conscious about the whiteness of our nearly naked bodies. When we felt the boys ogling our undeveloped breasts, we dissolved into fits of giggles.

Once, Jennifer's brother, Johnny, joined my brothers jumping at our bedroom window. I was most conscious of his gaze. Johnny was something else. When he was five, my brothers convinced him to steal candy from the local drugstore. Thrilled when the man at the register caught him, they rode home on their bicycles crowing "Johnny's coming home in a police car." Johnny's mother was standing in the doorway when a police cruiser drove up. His parents didn't ask what happened before Johnny proceeded to his bedroom and hid under the bed in shame. He didn't need to be punished.

One day after Dad died, Johnny's sister Jennifer arrived at our door carrying a large box of Barbie dolls, doll clothes and accessories. It didn't occur to me that Mom would be too proud to accept Jennifer's hand-me-downs. But she was. Enraged. Mad enough to find English words. "We no need charity!" she emerged from her dark bedroom where she now spent most of her days. She took the box of dolls out of my hands. "No need your garbage," shoving the box at Jennifer and slamming the door in her face. She could speak English! For the rest of the afternoon I could hear her behind her closed bedroom door, sputtering. "No good. Dirty garbage" as if practicing a language lesson. Jennifer never did come back into our home.

Johnny and I were in the same grade in high school. He was a science whiz, and I was almost pretty. We dated for a while. He invited me to our junior prom. For once I looked forward to dressing up for real. That spring I spent every evening at Jennifer and Johnny's house, a home as tidy as my house was chaotic. Johnny and I watched TV in his bedroom. His mother offered us bowls of vanilla ice cream.

We watched the Twilight Zone. We watched Star Trek. I sat next to him on his single bed with its white chenille bedspread. He kissed me, each kiss a tentative test, always asking me if I was okay. His touch was like respect.

I should never have told Kathy about the kiss. Kathy should never have told my mother (who understood a whole lot more than she let on). All I know is that one night, two weeks before prom; my mother was screaming in Japanese on the front walk of Johnny's immaculately maintained front yard with its pruned roses bushes and aroma of recently mowed grass. When Johnny's mother opened the door, her face became as white as my mother's was red.

As soon as I approached the door, my mother pounced on me, grabbing my arm and leaving a bruised outline of her fury. She pulled at me, yelling at Johnny: "Bad boy. Bad dirty boy." Pointing her finger emphatically. "Nasty boy!" I had never seen my mother so enraged; I had never heard her swear. "No garbage. My girl good. You bad boy, very bad boy." And a lot more in undecipherable Japanese words. Pointing and sputtering she pulled me away. I never went to the prom.

Five years later, Johnny and a friend invented the personal computer in his garage. Together, they started the company that changed the Valley forever. History was made thirty feet from my kitchen window.

One by one my siblings left. The boys asked for money to marry their girlfriends. Baby Joey went off to college in Oregon where he was still studying Asian languages when Mom passed away on Christmas Eve at the Pilgrim Haven nursing home. Joey never did talk with mom in her native language. She will always remain an enigma to us all.

I am glad that Mom was not around to learn about Eddie's shame. I believe in his innocence, just as I wish my mother had believed in mine that night at Johnny's. Eddie and I assumed our family's burden. How different my life might have been if Mom had not come between Johnny and me! I want to give Eddie the hope I was denied.

"Ready?" Eddie asks me. Eddie looks like my Dad. He has Dad's proud posture topped with Mom's jet black hair. Years of discipline and training have given him an air of confidence and strength. He is not a tall man but commands attention. Even his babies sit up taller when he enters the room.

The offices of Decker & LaFleur are sparkling clean, almost sterile with bright upholstery and framed pictures of the design for the new building being constructed for the Valley's most successful computer company. The headquarters' circumference will be nearly a mile around, a gleaming halo for the Valley. Kathy and Steve are already in the waiting room, flipping through magazines. Familiar faces in a foreign setting, a piece of home. The receptionist looks up. "So, we all here?"

Lydia LaFleur, our lawyer, awaits us at the end of a long wooden table in a room with windows looking out on the busy Cupertino crossroads. She sips from a cardboard Starbucks cup. "Have a seat. This won't take long." Straightening the color-coded file folders in front of her, she adds, "By the time we have gone over the paperwork, the Nguyens should be here and we should be all set." Lydia is perky. Her face unlined, her eyes wide. Her hair's blond highlights make her age hard to determine. She exudes confidence. "Can I offer you something to drink?"

Eddie asks for spring water. Lydia summons the receptionist and asks her to bring water. Lydia opens her folder.

"I've itemized the transaction here." She removes a sheet outlining the sales agreement and associated distributions. After the realtor's commission, taxes and lawyers' fees, there is enough left to pay off the mortgages and home loans. The balance I will receive is $405,258.

The numbers blur. I look at the address: 1319 Picaflor Lane. The address more familiar than my own aging face. Kathy and Mike are quiet. They do not ask to see the closing settlement, trusting as always that I will take responsibility. Uncomfortable in this cold corporate environment. Except for Eddie, who takes a long drink of water and swallows with a satisfied sigh.

"And my settlement?" he asked. "Is that here?" He is calm. He could take it or leave it. As if his life did not hang in the balance.

From the proceeds, I have agreed to pay $400,000 to satisfy all claims in the lawsuits against him. In exchange the parents of the children who accused him of abuse have agreed to drop all charges. This is what my Dad would have done.

Lydia nods. "Once the real estate transaction is complete, I have that paperwork." She picks up a second file. "We'll wire the funds by the end of the day."

And then I sign, page after page of X's. Kathy and Mike bear witness. As I sign, I recall each prior time the mortgages were refinanced: the gift of Mike's gas station, the houses bought for my brothers, the weddings, and Joey's college tuition. These pages, these numbers, calculate our family's story, once and for all to see. The celebrations, the heartbreaks and now one final rescue. I place the keys to the house on the polished wood of the conference table.

It is over. Eddie, Kathy, and Mike are already on their feet, looking relieved, pulling their smart phones from their pockets to check for messages.

In the waiting room the Nguyens have taken a seat on the couch where we sat moments before. This will be the first home for the young computer engineer and his pregnant wife, Lydia tells us, as she walks us to the door. They couldn't be more thrilled.

We ride down the one-floor elevator together. Kathy and Mike have left their car at his gas station and wave goodbye, walking away deep in private conversation. Eddie heads to the parking lot, his powerful stride energized with relief, his long legs already carrying him into a bright future. He forgets that he has given me a ride. I am left, standing alone at the busy intersection. On my right side, the atrium of the lawyers' office opens onto Starbucks where young people tap on their mobile devices, isolated in their own worlds. To the left, there is the Merrill Lynch "wealth management" store front with its air of exclusive elegance. Across the street the Hewlett Packard campus provides manicured shade. They leave me behind, without a ride home. It's a hot day and I am overdressed. I stand on the familiar corner waiting for Eddie to remember me.

Once, when I was ten, I rode my Schwinn bicycle through this same intersection on the way to the Safeway store. My mother sent me to pick up a bottle of milk and orange juice for the boys. As I approached the Shell gas station on the opposite corner, a blue Mustang pulled away from the pump. Maybe the driver was impatient or perhaps the attendant forgot to remove the gas nozzle from the car's fuel tank. Without warning, the underground storage tank and the Mustang exploded, shooting flames into the sky. In only seconds, the ball of fire was overshadowed by an enormous plume of black smoke. Waves of heat swept over me. Terrified, I peddled away, drawn as always to the safety of home.

Now I stand on that same corner and recall those distant flames. So much time has passed. Eddie has left me behind and will not remember to return to give me a ride. The smoke clears. I see the Nyugens exit the building, a happy family, hand in hand. I realize that I no longer belong here. The Valley that I have loved and the family that I have cherished have left me behind. Only the Johnnys belong here now.

SEE SOMETHING
SAY SOMETHING

The ringtone blasts like a gunshot, heavy metal taunting rap.

"Hey, man, wazzup." The smoker's voice, raspy. "Yeah, the bitch kicked me out."

On the other end, a distant voice: persistent, male.

"Accident or no accident, there's something wrong with that kid. She can't peg that on me."

The third car on the southbound Amtrak Vermonter is packed. Strangers, side by side, eyes glued to their devices. Fingers swiping headlines. iPods whispering in ears. The conductor walks the aisles, checking tickets, placing chits on overhead racks describing destinations up and down the East Coast. A recorded announcement plays over the loudspeakers: "Your safety is our first concern. If you see something, say something."

He is painfully slender, with a stubborn jawline. Julie had watched him walk down the aisle, loose-limbed, a marionette with slack strings. Worn jeans, flannel shirt, work boots scuffed. When he plops down beside her, she turns away, looking out the window at the receding city, lowering the shade halfway to block the glare of the winter sun. The train is inching out of Springfield, over the crumbling overpass and past the fitness club where treadmills overlook the tracks. She tries to ignore him.

Pulling out a book, she turns to the bookmark decorated with pressed flowers. She wrinkles her nose at his stale sweat, dirty jeans and the reek of tobacco. The narrator of her book has arrived in an exotic country, a radicalized nation on the State Department watch list, where she has holed up in a luxury hotel. Gazing out of her hotel-room window on the teeming street below, she is delaying the moment when she will venture out. The novel has not yet revealed her motivation.

He rubs his worn jeans, threads already stretched to the breaking point, the friction of calloused hands like kindling rousing a fire.

"Let her call the fucking police. I'm out of there. Who needs the aggravation? The bitch has real problems." He pokes his phone, ending the conversation. When the heavy metal ring resumes, he ignores the blast.

The heroine in her novel has ventured into the hotel lobby bar. Surrounded by a buffer of Americans in business suits, she orders a gin and tonic from the swarthy local bartender standing among potted palms. Outside the revolving glass doors of the hotel, armed guards hold locals at bay. Aromas from an open-air market waft in, spices and incense swallowed by the hotel's air conditioning.

He has a smoker's cough; sighs of exasperation plumb the pollution of his lungs.

Julie can't avoid exposure. Thinking of her heroine at the bar. How profiteers will risk danger whenever there is money to be made. Journalists who thrive on adrenalin as if, without it, they would dry up and die. What is the narrator's angle?

His fingernails are dirty; he has a laborer's hands. From the corner of her eye, she analyzes the grime, looking for clues to his predicament. He spreads out his legs and drifts off. She purses her lips, tries to breathe through her mouth, and waits for the momentum of the novel to pick up.

"Shit." He opens his eyes with a start. "Why are we stopped?"

The train is idling on a siding, waiting for the high-speed Acela to pass. He's slept through the conductor's garbled announcement that "the train will be moving shortly." Turning to him, she eyes the scratch marks on his face. Signs of a struggle? She sees him seeing her seeing him, doesn't ask for an explanation.

"Rough day." He rubs his eyes, looking her over, her navy pantsuit, the cleavage of her crisp white blouse, her book, her computer bag. "Man, I could use a drink." Picking up a greasy, battered backpack, he pulls out a pack of cigarettes like a dare and then settles for a stick of gum.

Calculating the consequences, she asks, "Where are you heading?"

"Right to hell," he answers, his sardonic laugh ending in a cough. "I feel like shit."

"Sorry to hear," she returns to her book, wishing that he would cover his mouth.

The novel's heroine lounges at the bar, comfortable among men. A professional woman, she is on a mission to recapture what she has nearly missed. In an orphanage high in the mountains, a baby waits for rescue. As she sips her drink, she studies a grainy photo, looking for a reflection in the foreign infant's dark eyes. Around her, journalists tell stories, a never-ending marathon of one-upmanship. She listens in mild amusement, knowing that their stories are two-thirds bullshit, one-third everything she aspires to be.

When the raucous ringtone reasserts itself, Julie tries to ignore it. The man beside her rouses himself to look at the display with scorn and then answers the phone impatiently.

"What?"

A woman's voice, loud and coarse. Julie hears urgency, repeated curses "...won't wake up," A pause. "...scared shitless." The angry voice loud enough to be heard over the distance. "What the hell have you done?" Another pause. "Do you hear me?"

Next to her, he is silent, eyes closed. He is listening but does not respond.

Julie can't help overhearing the tinny voice. "Joe, what the fuck? Where the hell are you?"

Pretending to read, she watches his reaction which is no reaction. A subtle clench of the jaw.

"I know you're there, you bastard."

Very gently, without making even the slightest noise, he closes the phone. Sighs.

The heroine turns over the baby's photo. There is no information on the back, not a name, not a birthdate. She has traveled far, but doubts remain. She worked hard work to accumulate the required funds for the adoption, but she cannot imagine how the baby's skin will feel, how she will hold the helpless infant. Easier to flirt with the businessman at her side, elicit the details of his recent negotiations with garment factory managers, sympathize with the challenge of making profit targets. Easier to signal her accessibility.

Joe stands up. "I need a beer," he announces to no one and heads off to the lounge car unsteadily, his legs almost spastic in their lack of control. When he returns, he holds a beer in one hand and his phone in the other. His backpack, slung over one shoulder, bangs against his bony hip. "Hey, dude," he bellows into the phone, "Guess who's coming to town. Want to party?" The last word drawn out like a proclamation.

The train has passed Hartford and is approaching New Haven. Julie watches as passengers shuffle in their seats, pack up their bags. Once again, the conductor announces that this is a full train and that additional passengers will board in New Haven where the line intersects with the regional train out of Boston. She sees an opportunity to change seats during the changeover. He has emptied one beer and pulls a second from his bag. Burping with dramatic enthusiasm, he pulls back the tab on the second can and turns to her, visibly more relaxed.

"That's more like it." Eyes without guile. "What's up, darling?"

The high rises of New Haven emerge from the wetlands. Graffiti covers overpasses. The train runs parallel to rush hour traffic on I-95, six lanes of commuters heading home. She gathers her belongings without indicating alarm, ready to grab the first empty seat. He grins at her. "Relax, sweetheart. We've got a long way to go." The "we" unsettles her. "New York, right?" As the train pulls into the station, he stretches his legs out like a gate, effectively trapping her in the window seat, daring her to protest. Before she can think of a valid excuse to flee, new passengers board. Empty seats fill. The train exchanges its diesel engine for electric and accelerates out of the station on its way through Connecticut towards New York.

Swallowing a disappointed sigh, she returns to her book. The back story is becoming clear. The narrator is reviewing correspondence with the orphanage, detailed instructions on bank transfers and emigration paperwork. The businessman to her right at the hotel bar watches her with curiosity, waiting for the opportunity to engage her once again in conversation, to slip his hand onto her thigh.

On the train, Joe continues to drink, melting into the dusty seat and spreading towards Julie as he relaxes into inebriation. Periodically, his phone fires off a summons, but he glances at the display and chooses not to answer. His head only a sliver from her shoulder, he inquires "Good book?"

Not capable of dismissing him as easily as he ignores his phone, she reads on, retaining nothing. Feeling trapped, she shifts to the right and looks out the window.

"Me, I prefer DVDs, a good shoot-'em-up with a chaser of pussy. Know what I mean?" He laughs and then coughs, laughs again.

She pulls herself erect, preparing to stand up for herself. She tries not to give into the tension his proximity evokes in her.

Tilting her head towards his phone, she says, "You're a popular guy."

With a guffaw, he answers, "You might say that." He gauges her reaction and then continues, "A bit of a mess. The girlfriend's a no-good crackhead on a bender. Don't know why I didn't ditch that mess a long time ago. Now her kid had an accident and she's going ballistic."

"Wow, that's rough," she says, wanting to hear more of the story, assess the blame.

"Yeah, it sucks," he says peremptorily, spitting a suspicion of beer her way. Skilled in his own way.

She refuses to get up, doesn't want to leave her belongings behind. The conductor passes by, collecting tickets from the newly boarded passengers. As he approaches her seat, he scans their receipts and continues. She cannot catch his eye.

In truth, she has seen nothing, has nothing to report but a vague sense of discomfort, distaste for tobacco smoke, an indescribable sense of challenge and threatened violation. He is a story she has skimmed without securing enough information for comprehension. A story she did not choose to read.

Again, the gunshots of his ringtone shake her. He looks at the phone's display and answers. "What?!" he demands again, this time indulging emotions that the beer has set free. "Go ahead. Call the fucking police. Good luck finding me." She hears sobs over the static and studies her book with great concentration, trying not to listen in on his conversation. The narrator has put away her legal papers and turns to the man next to her at the bar,

The baby wasn't a sure thing. The adoption agency had already received a large check but there remained the trip up the rocky, barren mountains in this dangerous, corrupt country where multiple factions demanded ransoms at make-shift roadblocks. The orphanage itself was a shady enterprise; the lineage of the babies suspect. The narrator has known this all along.

The voice on the phone doesn't know where Joe is. Why is she calling him instead of saving the child? Why isn't she taking responsibility? There are always two sides to a story. Julie wonders if Joe is the father of the crackhead's child. The situation sounds far from stable. The injuries described by the disembodied voice on the other end of his phone may have resulted from the mother's neglect, not abuse from the man at her side. The child's medical problems could have resulted from the irremediable damage so often seen in children born to drug addicts. As tragic as that might be, she finds it impossible to read the man beside her, to gauge his culpability and, as a result, her own responsibility.

Joe might be escaping the scene of a crime. If so, Julie's silence implicates her. If only he would go for more beer, she reasons, she could flag down the conductor, report the situation and clear her conscience. She sets her novel on her lap, hoping her calculation doesn't show. The train snakes through Connecticut suburbs, condos on one side, mansions skirting Long Island Sound on the other. BMWs and Mercedes crowd commuter lots. Cars back up on the parallel highway.

"Long trip?" she commiserates, looking for an angle. "Maybe you've got the right idea." She gestures at his beer can. His eyelids have gotten heavy. She does not want him to fall asleep.

"Always the right idea, sugar." His words slur; he ogles her cleavage.

She forces a smile, pulls out a ten-dollar bill. "Mind buying us a few more?" An offer she hopes he cannot refuse. She rises to the challenge of deceit.

Looking her over, he considers the proposal. She is careful not to hold her breath, reveal the obvious tell.

"Thank you, darling. Don't mind if I do."

He ambles down the aisle, bouncing from seat to seat. Mothers pull their children closer. Financiers close their laptops. She watches him, taking pride in her manipulation, the simplicity of her plan. She has become part of his story.

The conductor is nowhere in sight. Her time is limited. Leaving her bags unattended, she heads down the aisle in the opposite direction from the lounge car, looking for the conductor. She locates him sucking on a cigarette between passenger cars.

Approaching him, she points back to the car where she has been sitting. "The man beside me, two cars down, traveling from Vermont? I think he may be fleeing the police." She is breathless, unsure of herself. Never one to be dramatic, she struggles to appear calm but needs to capture his attention.

The conductor stomps out his cigarette. Well dressed, softspoken. She waits for him to evaluate her creditability.

"I overheard some phones calls. He may have harmed a child."

The conductor replies. "I'll call it in."

"Thank you, I appreciate it."

"See something, say something, right?" he chuckles. She wonders if he will follow through on the information, but she heads back to her seat. Joe has already returned and is thumbing through her novel. He makes no move to let her by and she is forced to climb over him. Face to face, he looks down her cleavage with a chuckle. "Any hoochie in this book?" Once she is seated, he hands her a beer she has no intention of drinking and drapes his arm around her. Her repulsion is colored by a heightened awareness of his touch, an unwelcome titillation. She grabs the book from him and struggles to read, his breath heavy in her ear.

The narrator is, indeed, about to have sex with the businessman. They have gone up to his hotel room where they share drinks from the mini bar. He has removed his polished shoes and stretches out on the king-size bed with an air of expectation. She unbuttons her blouse, no stranger to one-night stands. As he watches her undress, he discusses his negotiations, the greed of the locals who have no sense of the value of their wares. They will promise anything, he tells her, if the labor is cheap and exploitable. She commiserates.

Unable to concentrate on the page, Julie is conscious of Joe's body, the warmth of his arm resting on her back in a posture of reassurance that holds her captive at his side.

No sign of the conductor. Joe chuckles as he reads aloud from her book. "Removing her bra, he fondles her perky breasts, firm breasts that have never suckled a child." She blushes, embarrassed by the passage. The gritty reality of his voice reading into her ear paralyzes her, the warmth of his breath.

Stamford, Connecticut, approaches. High-rises, the headquarters of major financial institutions loom ahead like another world. She attempts push away Joe's exploring fingers. The afternoon sunshine flashes through the window, a confusing strobe that rattles her.

She slams the book shut. If the narrator had only focused on her journey, if she had headed out in search of her child as she had intended instead of dawdling at the hotel, this all might have gone down differently.

Joe's head rests on her shoulder.

Screeching brakes. Announcements overhead. Prep school students in grey blazers cluster on the platform. Stopped at the station, the train does not open its doors. Financiers grumble. Students shove each other with their shoulders and book bags.

Playfully sparring.

She sees policemen, two of them, walking down the platform toward their car. Joe, feigning sleep, is attempting to slip his dirty hand between her thighs. The conductor ushers a policeman up the stairs to their car. Struck by a sudden fear, she wonders if she has made this all up. Another fiction. Maybe the man beside her is nothing more than a lecherous nobody, amusing himself during a long, boring train ride. Is it possible she let her imagination run away with her? If so, she is about to be humiliated.

The cops enter the train to an audience of curious passengers. They head toward her. Joe opens his eyes, no sign of surprise, pulling her closer to him. Like a snake uncoiling, he removes his hand from her thigh and slips it into his grease-stained backpack. His drunken leer gone, he watches as the uniformed men approach.

"Joe Dean. Can we have a word with you?" The cop in charge is burly but well-manicured, a suburban cop used to treating citizens with respect.

"Who, me?" The cop bends over her, at ease, this moment another in a day of nuisance calls.

"I don't think you want to mess with me." The man locks eyes with the policeman, alert now, malevolent but thrilled by the attention. His hearts beats as quickly as her own. She looks straight ahead. Her book falls to the floor where it slams against the footrest. He holds her tight, the hand around her shoulders a warning. She tries not to swallow.

Around her, passengers rustle and whisper into their cell phones. She is not alone, she reminds herself. There are many witnesses. And yet, she feels vulnerable, defenseless.

"Hey, man." The cop attempts to defuse the situation, calm, a hint of a smile on his face. "So your girl..." he gestures toward her, "and you are having a little misunderstanding. Don't make things worse. I'm sure we can figure this out.'

She wants to remind them she is the one who reported him to the police. But she bites her tongue, knowing now is not the time to try and vindicate herself.

"Joe, we're here to take you home." As if this is a service he might appreciate. "Let it go, you can make this right."

Scoffing, Joe pulls her closer. She is almost in his lap now, her nostrils filled with fear and the smell of his rank sweat and alcohol. She looks at the back of the seat in front of her, struggles to maintain her composure, ignoring the bruise of his body against hers, concentrating on the roadblocks up the mountain that separate the narrator from the child that will fulfill her.

It was such garbage, all of it. The business dealings, the romance, the lies underlying it all. She stops listening to the cops' cautious entreaties, to Joe's surly responses. After this is over, she intends to dry clean her clothes. She will only read non-fiction and will always travel first class, regardless of the cost.

Additional police usher the passengers out of the car. As they pass by, they strain their necks to see the confrontation, already preparing to re-tell her story, their phones on speed dial, the tale taking on a life of their own. The seats clear out. Only she, he, and the police remain in a standoff.

Joe's phone again. The cops flinch at the jarring ringtone, their hands on their guns in readiness. Next time she will wear a turtleneck. What was she thinking that morning, dressing for her business trip, unbuttoning the button of her white blouse with every intention of using her femininity to persuade her boss to promote her?

She would have to reschedule the meeting.

His phone continues to fire.

"Joe, don't you think you should answer that?" the cop asks. "Maybe there is news about your son?" Her captor's muscles tighten, the jangle of the flight-or-fight response surging through his blood is audible. And then, without warning, he lets her go.

"What the hell." Joe puts his hands in the air, a well-rehearsed gesture, mocking the officials for the overkill of their response. "You win some, you lose some. Right, darling?" He winks at her as she touches her neck with a shaking hand. Almost tenderly, he adds, "But you've got to admit—this was the ride of your life!"

After they walk him down the aisle, she sits there collecting herself, admitting nothing.

How can she explain her role in the incident to the officer who remains at her side? She is this story's hero. Having seen something, she said something. The skeptical officer takes notes but offers no sympathy. "Why didn't you get up before the situation got out of hand?" he asks as he snaps his notebook shut.

In New York, she checks into her hotel room. She fills the bathtub with warm water, bubbles, and moisturizing salts. Despite her earlier resolution, she finishes the novel, enjoying the heartwarming denouement as she unwinds. She reads about the infant waiting when the narrator arrives at the orphanage after overcoming the expected obstacles, stronger for her pilgrimage. The baby girl's smile welcomes the mother who has arrived at last. Together, mother and child leave via a helicopter requisitioned by the one-night-stand businessman who just might become more, who had paid the necessary bribes and facilitated emigration paperwork.

She closes her eyes, trying to imagine the baby in the heroine's arms but instead all she sees is the man's face. She hopes his child is all right. Beside her, the novel slips into the warm water, taking on a life of its own, swelling all out of proportion. Stepping out on to the cold, tile floor, she swaddles her trembling body with the hotel's thick, white bath sheet.

It's only a story, she reminds herself, slipping into clean, crisp sheets. I am here, on my own, ready to make my case.

DOG DAYS

My kitchen is redolent with herbs. I'm knee deep in preservation, surrounded by carrots, cucumbers, and squash. Greens of all varieties, strawberries, radishes, and turnips. Three melons last week. Today, twenty- five tomatoes. A weekly task list dictated by my farm share, shaped by insect infestations and blight, rainfall totals.

At my feet, my dog Skylar is wasting away. She smells of old dog and is not uncomfortable. As long as she does not let me out of her sight, she is content Left alone she will howl and howl.

While I chop, my husband is helping our neighbor band birds. Every August, before the male ruby throated hummingbirds depart for points South, Ira and Roger spend an afternoon counting, measuring ,and banding the local hummingbird colony. The men hang a feeder, filled with sugar water in a birdcage, its door held open by a string which Ira grasps. When a bird enters, sucking sugar water to fatten up for his long journey south, Ira lowers the door.

Roger knows just how to handle the tiny birds. He checks for prior banding, measures the wings and beaks. Ira takes notes. Often the bird is repeat business, a frequent traveler. They make a note of which years he has been sighted, changes in his appearance.

How small my culinary efforts seem in light of a miniscule bird, barely larger than a butterfly about to make the journey to Florida, Texas, or Mexico. As my tomatoes simmer, Roger gives the final bird a reward of nectar and opens his palm. With a flutter of wings, his subject flies off into the August sky. I want to tag Skylar and wait for him to return to me.

Rogers's wife Beth is away on business. She does marketing for a large pharmaceutical company and flies all over the world to gauge markets. Roger and Beth chose not to have children. When Beth is home, we often hear their arguments over the fence; they have knock down drag out fights which culminate in tears and amorous evenings in their backyard Jacuzzi.

I am expecting my second child. My first, Sam, is a happy toddler with his father's easy joy. Last night Ira practiced catching hummingbirds with him, showing him how to hold the bird in his small hand. They made a model out of green Legos and Sam held his precious cargo so tenderly that it brought tears to my eyes. I want to give him everything. I don't want him to see Skylar die.

Maybe it's the hormones. I have been remembering my mother sprawled out drunk on the bathroom floor one summer during my college vacation. A contentious summer. My mother, a corporate lawyer, lived to prove her worth. My brother and I were a reflection of her, our report cards her measure. She spent that summer enumerating my many shortfalls: my mediocre grades, my poor choice of major, my weight gain, my inability to find a proper boyfriend.

I tried it once. Drinking enough vodka that I didn't feel anything. It didn't work.

"At least I will never be like you." I screamed, slamming the door. Out of there for good.

"Don't expect me to pay your tuition next year." She yelled after me.

That's when I flew away. I became a college dropout, my mother's worst nightmare.

It would be years before I found another relationship with as much intensity as that I had with my mother. Ira and I wear kid gloves, even now. We have vowed to be careful with each other.

I chop vegetables. My pantry is almost full. After putting away his gear, Roger joins us on our deck looking out into the woods over glasses of Chardonnay. He describes the thrill of the hummingbird's heart throbbing in his palm. As we eat overflowing bowls of salad full of fresh farm greens, we identify bird calls: the jays' screech, the thrushes' waterfall. Sam searches for butterflies in the fields, telling our cat about the days' adventure. He is already synthesizing the experience, making it his own.

The end of summer is in sight.

Roger's phone rings and he walks to the edge of the field to answer it. When Beth is away, Roger is calmer. He visits often and throws sticks for Skylar. But he keeps his phone close, his lifeline to his wife. Beth is flying home from Thailand tonight.

Roger's face is pale when he returns.

"What's up?" Ira asks. We assume that they have had another argument and are ready to sympathize as always. We are old hands at this. Later we analyze. We are voyeurs of their passion, borrowing the intensity without the pain.

"It's gone." I can almost not hear him. As if he lacks the strength to form the words. I look over at Sam, watch to be sure Skylar is still breathing.

"What's gone?" Ira gets up and puts an arm around his friend.

"Her plane. It just disappeared off the radar screen."

Ira stands there with his hands open, entreating. These things don't happen. He is a scientist waiting for a logical explanation. We listen, but all we can hear is the breeze in the trees and the distant gurgle of the stream. I take Sam's hand. Skylar stretches out on the deck, his ribs rising and falling faintly. We walk into the lighted house and I look back at the two men and the old dog in the darkness. The sun goes down early these days.

My mother and I talk once a month now, long distance. She asks about my son but makes no effort to visit. I post photos on Snapfish but she seldom comments on them. She does not understand why I would want to live in the country. "What do you do all day alone at home?" she asks. I describe the little things, pushing my son on a rope swing, watching him do his first puzzles, baking pies with fruit we have picked during the afternoon's walk.

Now I think. They will find the plane.

Ira and Roger have gone to his study to call the airlines. I hear CNN in the background. The newscaster is describing the routine flight, the experienced pilot who had signed off as he exited Thailand's airspace at nightfall. There was no indication anything was wrong, they repeat. The TV screen flashes in the dark room. I listen to Roger sob, hear Ira comforting him, his voice soft and gentle.

The plane disappeared with 245 passengers aboard.

"Do you remember when I taught you how to drive?" My mother asked me last month. She reminded me that she was the parent with enough patience to hold her breath when I turned too sharply, landing on our carefully manicured front lawn. She said we laughed about it later, saying that if we had driven into the living room we could have announced "We're home!" I remember her tight-lipped, the guttural noises in her throat when I stopped too quickly. How she braced herself against the dashboard.

She says she wants to be present for the baby's birth.

It occurs to me that we all reinvent our past.

More foolishly, we pretend to control the future.

My baby kicks. I hope it is a girl.

I know they won't find the airplane.

I read Sam a good night story, my ears pealed for news from the next room. I love holding him in my lap, the way he snuggles in, his soft hair tickling my neck. He asks me questions about hummingbirds, how they fly. He describes the beating of their wings, bats his eyes to show how fast. He describes Roger placing the bands, letting him touch the stunned birds. In his version, Roger is calm and in control and life is amazing. I want to freeze these moments for him before he succumbs to a world that is careening out of control. I want him to remember this, bonds this simple, this pure. I want to shield him from the sorrow in our home.

I wonder how Roger will live without Beth. Which will he miss more, the battles or the passionate lovemaking? The Jacuzzi in his back yard breaks my heart.

What is my mother thinking, asking to be present at the birth? How will she handle the mess of it all? The blood and gore of delivery? Will she need a drink? Will she and Sam stand together and watch as the midwives pull my baby into the world?

When I was a girl, my mother would play the radio while she cleaned the house "I am woman. Hear me roar." She would strut across the living room pushing the vacuum like a bayonet. I never questioned what it took for my mother to be the primary wage earner in our family. I only held her accountable for her absences, her inability to "get" me. All the tools she offered me seemed wrong. The cherries she gave me from her manhattans were poisonous.

Now I am afraid of her flying. Afraid of having to reinvent her once again.

Soon the hummingbirds will be gone. It's an endless cycle. It is an illusion that we can count on them returning. How can 245 people disappear into the Atlantic Ocean while a minute ruby throat makes its annual journey to Mexico unscathed? How can I dare to bring a child into this world and let my mother bear witness after fleeing from her in order to begin my life?

I feel a fluttering in my womb, already bracing for flight. Banded by me out of curiosity and a desire for evidence of my care. Will I have the chance to teach this child how to pick the fresh herbs from a summer garden? Can I teach her how to preserve sustenance for the dark times? Will she be able to forgive me?

I warm water for tea and set out the peach cake on the kitchen table knowing it will offer little solace this dark night. Gestures are all we have. Food is as primal as we get. Sam is asleep with Skylar at his feet. The dog twitches as he runs through some dream field, young again. Roger has not set down his silent phone. We sit up all night, watching TV coverage, the endless loop of information that is not known, unable to turn off the anchor's morbid fascination. When the sun rises, we are already older.

As Roger pulls out of our driveway, I think: perhaps Skylar and I will wander the U-pick fields together before she dies, Maybe my mother will join us. When winter comes it will be too late. The dog's heart will give out. My mother will change her mind. Roger will be a widower with a white untanned ring around his finger.

But my freezer will be full. When winter buries the farm

fields, the vegetables I have chopped will still be there, frozen or dried or packed in salt. During the darkest days, my pantry will overflow.

My farmers plan their spring crops in January. They draw maps and calculate demand. Like the flash of a ruby throat about to depart, the season in almost gone. Now is the time to prepare for the unforeseeable future.

Acknowledgement

Several of these stories appeared in somewhat different forms in literary journals. Shoes was published by The Adirondack Review in 2016, Stalking the Beatles was published by Calliope Magazine in 2015, and Dog Days was included in Juno Esq Literary Journal in 2015. Thanks to these editors for publishing my work.

The story Real Estate continued to grow and evolve, morphing into the novel Real Estate, published by Propertius Press in 2020. The story, The Cost of Electricity is undergoing a similar transformation.

Finally, I'd like to thank my Amherst Co-Housing writing group, the Green Mountains Writers Conference, my good friend Marianne Gambaro, and my always encouraging and supportive husband. Lew, for their support, patience, and editing skills.

In the words of the Beatles, Love is all you need. No matter where you are, whatever the era, family and friends provide the best inspiration.

ABOUT THE AUTHOR

Kathryn Holzman

After attending Stanford University and
NYU, Kathryn Holzman chose Health Care
Administration as a career, working with
public inebriates, dentists, urologists, and
cardiologists. When the right side of her
brain rebelled against endless databases
and balance sheets, she returned to her first
passion—fiction. Her short fiction has ap-
peared in over twenty online literary maga-
zines and print anthologies. She is the author of a collection
of short fiction, FLATLANDERS, Shire Press 2019 and the novel
REAL ESTATE. Propertius Press, Fall 2020. She was awarded the
Grand Prize in the 2020 Eyelands International Short Story Con-
test. Links to her work can be found at kathrynholzman.com.

BOOKS BY THIS AUTHOR

Flatlanders

Kathryn Holzman's collection of short fiction explores the truce between Vermont's homesteaders and the second-home owners who co-exist in the lush Green Mountains. Vermont's motto, Freedom and Unity might lack the bombastic glory of New Hampshire's declaration, Live Free or Die, but it captures the Vermont spirit of stubborn cooperation. Whether sharing a blackberry patch with a bear or dropping off garbage at the local transfer station, life in Vermont unites its disparate residents in surprising ways.

Real Estate (Propertius Press 2020)

REAL ESTATE is the story of how a bucolic agricultural valley is transformed into the iconic Silicon Valley.

As acres of apricot orchards are sold off to create suburban subdivisions, families flock to the area. Air Force pilot Joe Jackson moves his family to Sunnyvale soon after the Hopkins build their dream house next door. Harriet and Bobby share a side-yard fence, but the worlds they live in differ radically. Nevertheless, a shared fascination with the Beatles and the loss of the inspiring young President Kennedy bring them together in an unlikely friendship.

As the valley evolves into an affluent center of engineering technology, their family's differences widen and eventually tear them apart. While Harriet struggles to fulfill family obligations. Bobby builds a computer in his garage. In the valley, both Harriet and Bobby learn that family is not always destiny and houses are sometimes more than a home.